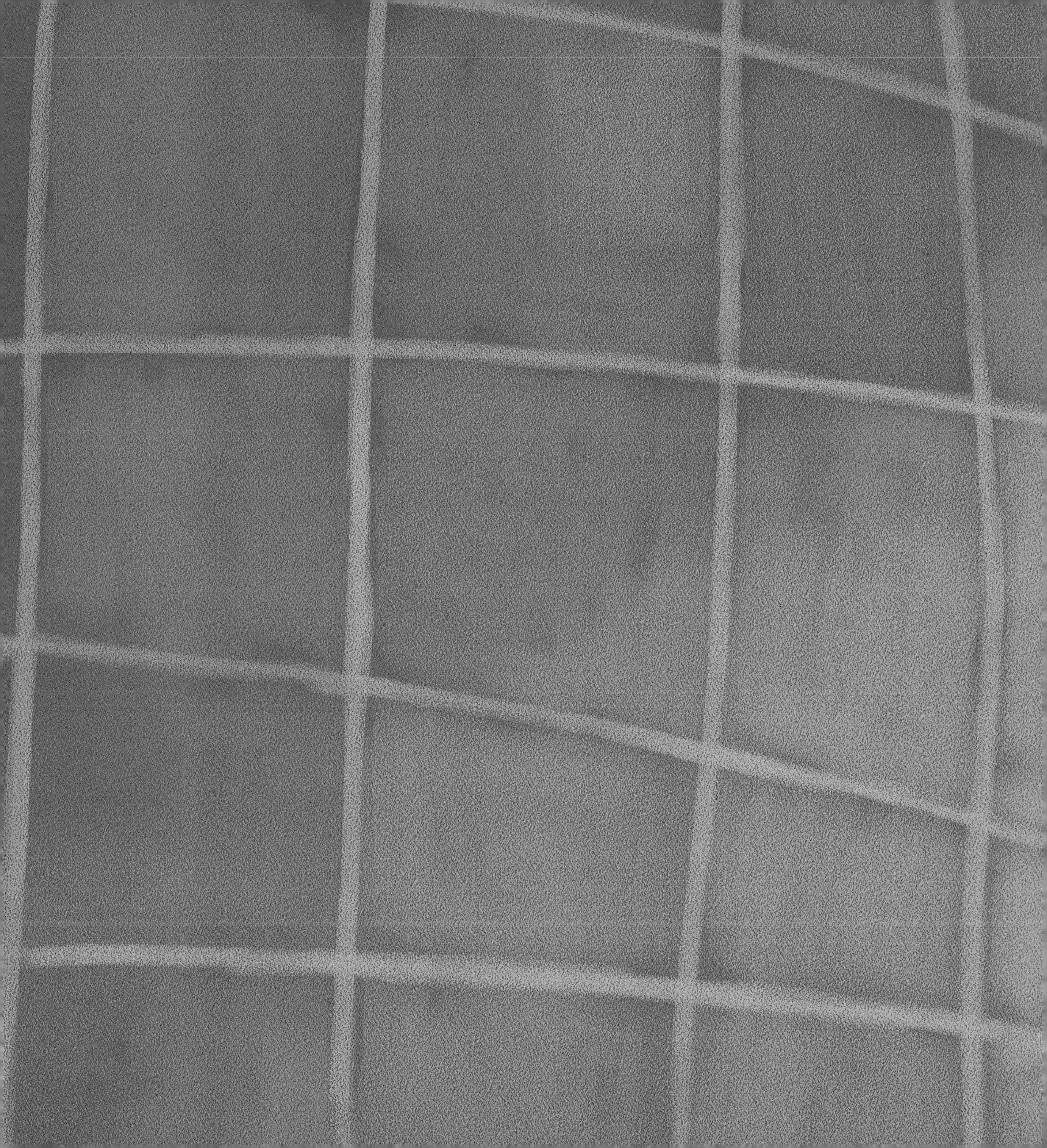

Published by Top That! Publishing plc
Tide Mill Way, Woodbridge, Suffolk, IP12 1AP, UK
www.topthatpublishing.com

0 2 4 6 8 9 7 5 3 1
Printed and bound in China

Creative Director – Simon Couchman
Editorial Director – Daniel Graham

Written by Gordon Volke
Illustrated by The Fénix Factory

ISBN 978-1-84956-305-5

A catalogue record for this book is available from the British Library
Printed and bound in China

Hullabaloo!

Written by Gordon Volke

There's a donkey called Drew
Making a **hullabaloo** at the zoo.

There's a cockatoo who squawks out 'Boo!'
And a donkey called Drew
Making a **hullabaloo** at the zoo.

The chimp twins, Daisy and Maisie, enjoy their tea-for-two,
With the cockatoo who squawks out 'Boo!'
And a donkey called Drew
Making a **hullabaloo** at the zoo.

There are hopping bunnies with lots of grass to chew,
While the chimp twins, Daisy and Maisie, enjoy their tea-for-two,
With the cockatoo who squawks out 'Boo!'
And a donkey called Drew
Making a **hullabaloo** at the zoo.

There's a calf called Cassie who keeps on saying 'Moo!'
And hopping bunnies with lots of grass to chew,
While the chimp twins, Daisy and Maisie, enjoy their tea-for-two,
With the cockatoo who squawks out 'Boo!'
And a donkey called Drew
Making a **hullabaloo** at the zoo.

There are downy ducklings marching through!
Past a calf called Cassie who keeps on saying 'Moo!'
And hopping bunnies with lots of grass to chew,
While the chimp twins, Daisy and Maisie, enjoy their tea-for-two,
With the cockatoo who squawks out 'Boo!'
And a donkey called Drew
Making a **hullabaloo** at the zoo.

There's a roo called Sue with her joey, Blue,
who bounce around (that's all they do!)
And downy ducklings marching through!
Past a calf called Cassie who keeps on saying 'Moo!'
And hopping bunnies with lots of grass to chew,

While the chimp twins, Daisy and Maisie, enjoy their tea-for-two,
With the cockatoo who squawks out 'Boo!'
And a donkey called Drew
Making a **hullabaloo** at the zoo.

There are baby owls who sit and say 'Twit-to-woo!'
Beside a roo called Sue with her joey, Blue,
who bounce around (that's all they do!)
And downy ducklings marching through!
Past a calf called Cassie who keeps on saying 'Moo!'
And hopping bunnies with lots of grass to chew,
While the chimp twins, Daisy and Maisie, enjoy their tea-for-two,
With the cockatoo who squawks out 'Boo!'
And a donkey called Drew

Making a **hullabaloo** at the zoo.

There's a hungry goat whose horns are all askew,
There are baby owls who sit and say 'Twit-to-woo!'
Beside a roo called Sue with her joey, Blue,
who bounce around (that's all they do!)
And downy ducklings marching through!
Past a calf called Cassie who keeps on saying 'Moo!'
And hopping bunnies with lots of grass to chew,
While the chimp twins, Daisy and Maisie, enjoy their tea-for-two,
With the cockatoo who squawks out 'Boo!'
And a donkey called Drew

Making a **hullabaloo** at the zoo.

Don't forget Dapple the horse – we must include him too!
There's a hungry goat whose horns are all askew,
There are baby owls who sit and say 'Twit-to-woo!'
Beside a roo called Sue with her joey, Blue,
who bounce around (that's all they do!)
And downy ducklings marching through!
Past a calf called Cassie who keeps on saying 'Moo!'
And hopping bunnies with lots of grass to chew,
While the chimp twins, Daisy and Maisie, enjoy their tea-for-two,
With the cockatoo who squawks out 'Boo!'
And a donkey called Drew

Making a **hullabaloo** at the zoo.

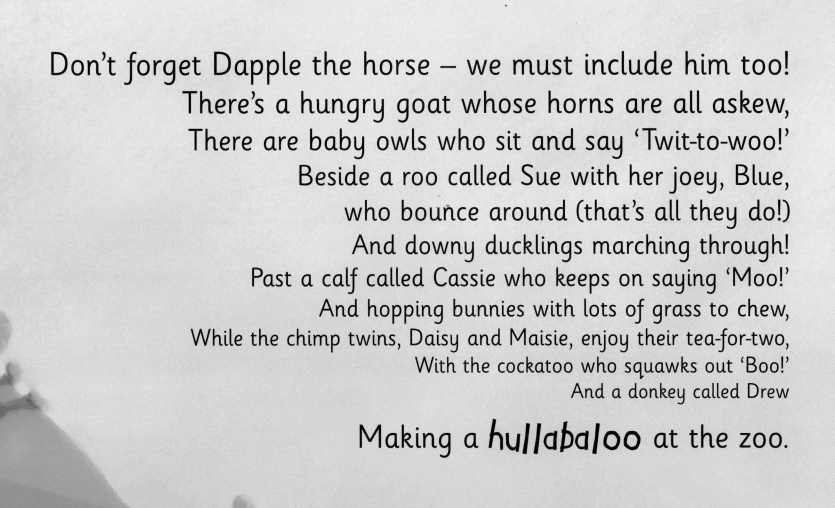

There's someone missing from the

hullabaloo at the zoo!

Who?

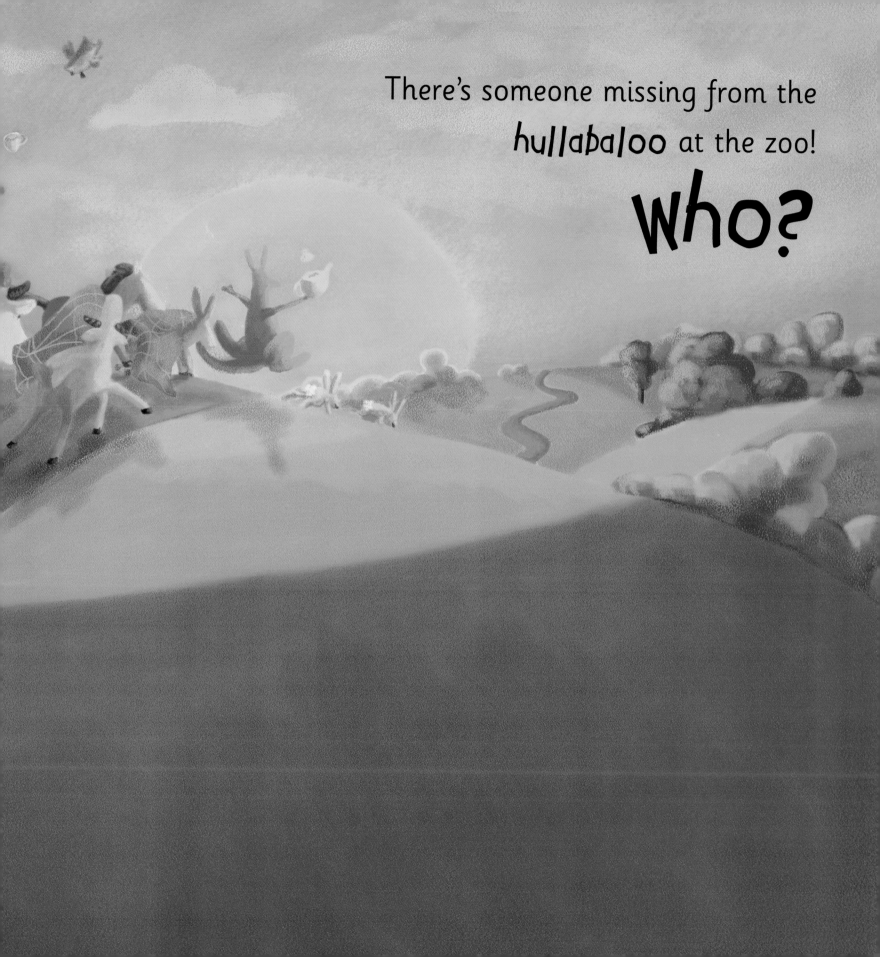

You!

THE END

Boo!

More great picture books from Top That! Publishing

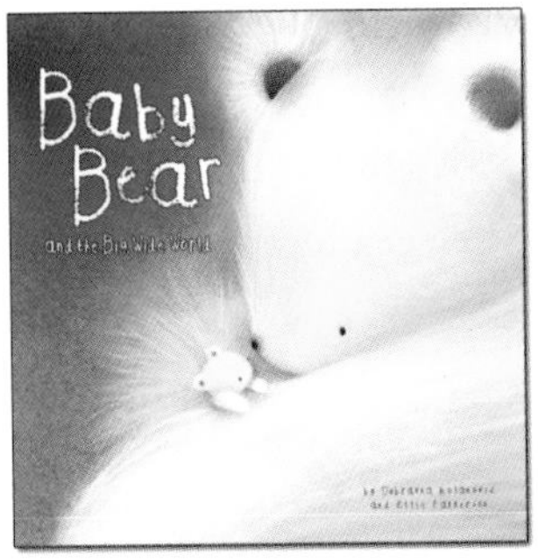

ISBN 978-1-84956-120-4

Baby Bear tentatively explores the wonders of the outside world.

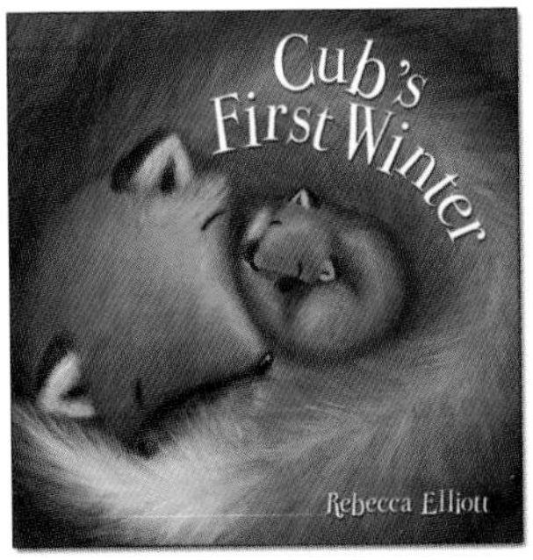

ISBN 978-1-84956-099-3

An inquisitive fox cub experiences the onset of his first winter.

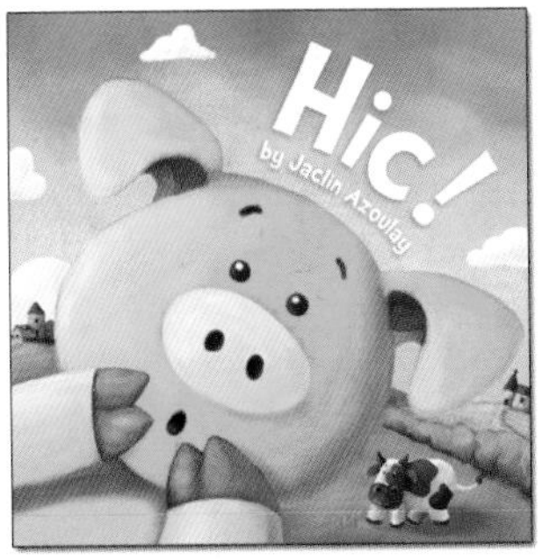

ISBN 978-1-84956-303-1

Snuffletrump the piglet will try anything to get rid of his hiccups!

ISBN 978-1-84956-073-3

Can you find Hiku as he sneaks away from an important family visit?

ISBN 978-1-84956-305-5

The animals are making a hullabaloo in this humorous picture storybook!

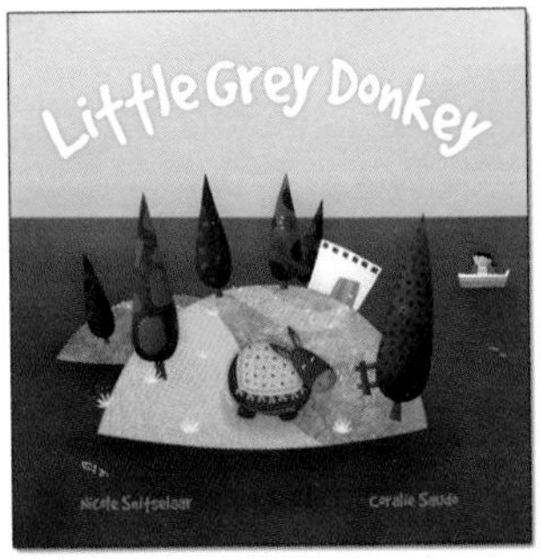

ISBN 978-1-84956-245-4

Unique illustrations capture the loving bond between two best friends!

ISBN 978-1-84956-304-8

Milly the meerkat learns a very important lesson in this classic tale.

ISBN 978-1-84956-302-4

Follow the antics of the escaped zoo animals as they cause pandamonium!

ISBN 978-1-84956-101-3

Enjoy the beautiful moments between a mother cat and her kitten.

ISBN 978-1-84956-100-6

Comic wordplay explores what a toucan or toucan't do.

Available from all good bookstores or visit www.topthatpublishing.com

Look for Top That! Apps on the Apple iTunes Store